W9-BRD-292

PETER AND THE WOLF

DESIGNED AND ILLUSTRATED BY WARREN CHAPPELL· CALLIGRAPHY BY HOLLIS HOLLAND

PETER AND THE WOLF

SERGE PROKOFIEFF

WITH A FOREWORD BY
SERGE KOUSSEVITZKY

SCHOCKEN BOOKS · NEW YORK

First published by Schocken Books 1981
10 9 8 7 6 5 4 3 2 1   81 82 83 84
Published by arrangement with Alfred A. Knopf, Inc.

Copyright © 1940 by Alfred A. Knopf, Inc.

Library of Congress Cataloging in Publication Data
Prokofiev, Serge, 1891–1953. Peter and the wolf. The narration with musical
themes. Reprint. Originally published: New York : Knopf, 1940. Summary: Retells
the orchestral fairy tale of the boy who, ignoring his grandfather's warnings,
proceeds to capture a wolf. [1. Fairy tales] I. Chappell, Warren, 1904–   ill. II. Title.
PZ8.P947 1981   [E]   81–40404 AACR2

Manufactured in the United States of America
ISBN 0–8052–0684–1

The absorbing orchestral narrative, PETER AND THE WOLF, has the charm and simplicity of all great fairy tales. Written primarily for children, its appeal is universal. The enthusiastic acclaim with which the general public greeted my performances with the Boston Symphony Orchestra, of this strangely moving tale, was startling. The continued growing interest in PETER AND THE WOLF among adults, is especially gratifying to me.

I am so happy that my good friends, Blanche & Alfred Knopf, have made it possible for adults as well as children to enjoy this beautiful fairy tale. The unusual illustrations have captured the feeling of this truly delightful story which Prokofieff expressed so humorously in music.

Serge Koussevitzky

Early one morning Peter
opened the gate and went out
into the big green meadow. On
the branch of a birch tree sat

Early one morning Peter opened the gate and went out into the big green meadow.

a little bird, —Peter's friend. When he saw Peter he chirped at him gaily, "All's quiet here."

Soon a duck came waddling around. She was very happy to see that Peter had not closed the gate, and so decided to have a nice swim in the deep pond in the meadow. As soon as the

little bird saw the duck, he flew
down and settled himself in
the grass beside her. Shrugging
his shoulders he said, "What
kind of a bird are <u>you</u> if you
can't fly?" To which the duck
replied, "What kind of a bird
are <u>you</u> if you can't swim?"
and dived into the pond.

On the branch of a birch tree sat a little bird, — Peter's friend

Soon, a duck came waddling around _____.

They argued and argued, the
duck swimming in the pond,

the little bird hopping back and forth along the bank. Suddenly, something caught Peter's eye.

It was a cat crawling through the grass. The cat said to herself, "The bird is busy arguing. If I could only have him for my

MODERATO

con eleganza

dinner!" Stealthily she crept toward him on her velvet paws. "Oh, look out!" cried Peter.

It was a cat crawling through the grass.

Quickly the bird flew up into
the tree while the duck quacked
angrily at the cat —from the

middle of the pond. The cat
crawled round and round the
tree and thought, "Is it worth
climbing up so high? By the
time I get there the bird will
have flown away."

All at once Grandpapa came out. He was angry because Peter had gone to the meadow. "The meadow is a dangerous place," he cried. "What if a wolf should

come out of the forest?—What would you do then?" Peter paid no attention to Grandpapa's words.

All at once, Grandpapa came out.

Boys like Peter are not afraid
of wolves. Grandpapa took
Peter by the hand, led him home
— and locked the gate.

No sooner had Peter gone than
a big grey wolf _did_ come out
of the forest. In a twinkling
the cat sprang up into the tree.
The duck quacked and in her
great excitement, jumped out
of the pond.

No matter how hard the duck tried to run, she couldn't escape the wolf. He was getting nearer and nearer. He was catching up with her—there—he got her — and swallowed her with a single gulp!

A big grey wolf did come out of the forest.

And now this is how things stood:
the cat was sitting on one branch up in
the tree,—the bird was sitting on another,
—not too close to the cat,—while the wolf
walked round and round the tree, look-
ing at them both with greedy eyes. In
the meantime, Peter, without the slight—
est fear, stood behind the closed gate,
watching all that was going on. Present-
ly, he ran into the house, found a strong
rope, hurried back and climbed up the
high stone wall. One of the branches of
the tree around which the wolf was pac-

ing, stretched out over this high wall. Grabbing hold of this branch, Peter climbed over into the tree. He said to the bird, "Fly down and circle around the wolf's head, but take care that he doesn't catch you!" The bird almost touched the wolf's head with his wings, while the wolf snapped furiously at him from this side-and that. How that bird did worry the wolf! And oh! how the wolf tried to catch him! But the bird was far too clever for him.

Meanwhile, Peter had made a lasso, and

letting it down very carefully–he caught the wolf by the tail and pulled with all his might. Feeling himself caught, the wolf began to jump wildly, trying to get loose. But Peter had tied the other end of the rope to the tree, and the wolf's jumping only made the rope tighter around his tail! Just then, who should come out of the woods but the hunters who were

Who should come out of the woods but the hunters.

following the wolf's trail, and shooting
as they came. From his perch in the tree
Peter cried out to them: "You don't need
to shoot. The bird and I have already
caught him! Please help us take him
to the zoo."

The hunters were only too willing. And
now you can just imagine the triumphant

procession! Peter at the head – after him the hunters, leading the wolf — and winding up the procession, Grandpapa and the cat. Grandpapa shook his head reprovingly. "This is all very well, but what if Peter had <u>not</u> caught the wolf, – what then!" Above them flew the little bird, merrily chirping, "Aren't we smart, Peter and I? See what <u>we</u> have caught!" And if you had listened very carefully, you could have heard the duck quacking away inside the wolf, because in his haste the wolf had swallowed her whole – and the duck was still alive.

And now, you can just imagine the triumphant procession

. . . the little bird, merrily chirping, "Aren't we smart, Peter and I?"

Each character of this Tale is represented by a corresponding instrument in the orchestra: Peter by the string quartet,

 the bird by the flute,

 the duck by the oboe,

 the cat by the clarinet in a low register,

 the grandfather by the bassoon,

 the wolf by three horns,

 the shooting of the hunters by the kettle and bass drums.